My Guardian Anger

Steve Cain

ISBN: 9798839891999

More from Steve Cain:

The Great Inevitable, Losantiville Press
Jumpin' Jesus, Hallelujah, Amazon
Thorn, Amazon
The Box of Dreams and Memories, Amazon,
Leave a Message, Amazon,
December Promise, Amazon
The Crown and the Harp, Amazon
Nothing but Sand, Amazon
Dead Birds, Amazon
Bombs and Dragons, Amazon

DEDICATION

My Guardian Anger is dedicated to John Patrick McDonald, also known as Midnight, who was the lead singer for the band Crimson Glory. Midnight, you have been my muse and a huge influence on my singing and writing. Your memory remains. It never really ends.

CONTENTS

My Guardian Anger

ACKNOWLEDGMENTS

I would like to thank all of you who have taken the time to read my works, especially the ones who have been with me from the beginning. If you have *The Great Inevitable,* you know who you are. Peace and love to you all. I appreciate you!

Author's Note

Hey there! What's up? Thank you for stopping by! You could be reading Stephen King or Charles Dickens, Shakespeare or Poe, James Patterson or Brad Meltzer right now, but you have MY book open! Wow! Thank you!

My Guardian Anger was written between November 2021 and December 2021. For some reason, probably the holidays, I had a pretty good writing spurt going on. The holidays are a great time, but they're also bittersweet, thinking about my parents and old holiday memories, etc.

This is my 11th book. I'm proud of all of them. Like my kids, my books are my children. I love them. This particular book is solely poetry. I never set out to be a poet, but here I am. It's what's in my head. It's what's in my heart. It's what's in my soul. I always thought I'd be a novelist, and maybe I will be one day after I retire from my day job. You know work always gets in the way!

If you are so inclined, please check me out on Facebook. My page is Steve Cain Writer. You can also check out my Christian metal band, Wars and Rumors, on Facebook. We are busy writing and rehearsing to record a CD and to play live in the fall. Please connect with me; I love interacting with people. I hope to see you at a show!

Steve, 7/6/2022

My Guardian Anger

Shaking,

And the blood is boiling

Deep down inside.

Racing,

And my heart is thumping.

I can no longer hide.

Screaming,

Howls streaming out,

Mouth wipe open.

Scheming,

Plotting revenge,

I wish you'd died,

But…

Finally,

I have my chance.

Finally,

No looking back.

My guardian anger,

Surface,

My rage and pain.

My guardian anger,

Lurking,

Inside my brain,

Insane.

Violence

Is taking me over,

Embracing me.

Righteous,

Controlling my thoughts and

Controlling me.

Silence,

My screaming is over,

My focus on now,

Trigger,

Alarms are sounding.

My will is gone,

But…

Finally,

I have my chance.

Finally,

No looking back.

My guardian anger,

Surface,

My rage and pain.

My guardian anger,

Lurking,

Inside my brain,

Insane.

Finally.

Finally.

Finally.

Finally.

My guardian anger,

Surface,

My rage and pain.

My guardian anger,

Lurking,

Inside my brain.

My guardian anger,

Surface,

My rage and pain.

My guardian anger,

Lurking,

Inside my brain,

Insane.

In my brain.

Insane.

In my brain.

Insane.

By the Midnight Moon She Comes

Shadows pass me overhead.

The owls and crickets grow silent.,

But somewhere in the distance,

A lone coyote brays.

By the midnight moon she comes,

Lies beside me on a flannel blanket,

And coaxes me into her arms,

Again.

Dark hair falls across my bare chest,

And I feel the coldness in her breath,

Her frigid touch.

I can smell the earth upon her skin,

And I die again and again.

I die again and again.

1000 Devils

100 devils haunt me,

Torture me,

Confound me in the night.

1000 devils,

With torn and blackened wings,

Long, sharp talons,

Serrated rapiers,

Instruments of torture.

They scream in ancient lies,

Spewing venom and curses.

How they strike at me night after night,

After my soul!

They promise pain,

Torments inconceivable.

They laugh when they speak my name.

1000 devils.

1000 angels,

Descending from heaven,

Bathed in golden light,

Sparkling white wings,

Flaming two-edged swords.

They join in the battle,

Fighting back the devils,

Whispering love in my ears as they slash at my tormentors.

Quickly,

With little trouble at all,

My angels drive the devils away,

And I am saved.

Then,

In another flash of blinding light,

My protectors are gone,

And a single white feather lands on the pillow next to my head.

I can sleep in comfort again,

Until tomorrow,

When 1000 devils will return,

And the battle will begin again.

Praying for Rain

Sitting on the porch,

And something's missing,

Just holding a cup of coffee in my hands.

The warmth feels good,

The steam rising up,

Warm in my nostrils.

Something's missing.

I wish it would rain.

The sky is gray,

And the temperature's dropped.

The clouds are threatening,

But it's just a tease.

That's what the weatherman says,

And you know he's never wrong.

I'm praying, though,

Praying for rain.

I will run out and stand,

Arms wide open,

And I will get cleansed

It's what I need.

It's what I need

Because the tears are not enough,

For they are tainted, too.

I could fill up a tub with my tears,

But they won't wash away my stains.

Rain on me,

Please.

I'm praying.

I need it.

Make me clean again.

<u>War March Fly</u>

It comes to this:

War!

It was inevitable,

Don't you think?

All the treachery,

The greed,

The backstabbing.

The lies,

The deceit.

It is war!

I will march with my army,

You with yours,

And we will fly at each other,

Have at each other,

With bayonets,

Swords,

Bullets,

Fists.

Rage,

Hate,

Betrayal,

Pain,

Brother!

We will spill our blood on this battlefield!

March!

Fly!

Tears,

Blood,

Rain,

Mud,

Saliva,

Vomit.

This ground will never be pure again;

The ghosts of war will haunt this field for a thousand years,

Brothers fighting brothers in our unholy names!

See what you've done?

You've damned them!

You've damned them all!

You damned us.

It should be you that falls in this field,

You that gets his eyes plucked out,

His bones picked over by the turkey vultures!

It should be you,

But you are a coward!

Don't run!

Turn around and face me!

The blood is thick,

The mud is thin,

Like my patience.

Brother,

Let me see your face.

Brother,

Let me see the red of your eyes.

See the hate and the pain in the curl of my lips?

You may run,

But these ghosts won't let you get away.

The ghosts on both sides of this war,

They know that you're to blame,

Your hubris,

Your envy.

They know you killed them,

And I will be their revenge!

You're going nowhere,

And neither am I.

War, march, fly!

War, march, fly!

See the flash of my blade through the drops of rain;

It won't be the last thing you see.

My eyes,

Those are what you'll see as you take your last breath,

As I pull the sword from your guts.

It should never have come to this.

Father,

Forgive me.

I know what I do,

And I do it anyway.

March,

Brothers!

March,

Ghosts!

It's time to end this.

It's time to end this.

It's time to rest.

The Bond

I can see your eyes sparkling in the darkness of our room.

I can see your fingers resting beneath your chin.

I can hear the music in your breath

And the rhythm of your heartbeat.

I can taste the salt on your skin,

The salt in your tears.

I feel the silk in your hair

And the satin in your touch.

I can smell the coconut lotion on your body

And the hint of cherries on your breath.

Your soul calls to me,

And I answer.

This is where Dream,

Memory,

And Life melt together.

This is our love.

This is our bond.

<u>Champ</u>

Champ,

I barely remember you.

Champ,

I am not really sure I remember you at all,

Champ,

But I have a picture,

A picture somewhere,

Of you and I together,

And I was smiling,

And you looked happy.

You must've been a good boy.

You must have been a good boy.

I'm sure I loved you,

Champ.

I'm sure I missed you,

Champ.

You must've been a good boy.

Somewhere Far from Here

Streetlamp shining down,

And she's smoking a cigarette,

Waiting for a ride that'll never come.

Neon signs flash,

A hamburger joint,

A tattoo parlor,

Emory's Liquor.

The neon lights illuminate her makeup,

Half applied, rushed.

Flash on,

Flash off,

Flash on again.

There's a hot dog vendor on the corner,

And he sneaks peeks as he slaps on mustard and onions.

The smell never washes off completely.

There is lust and amusement in his eyes.

She is not for him,

But one can dream.

Around the corner and down the street,

A police siren wails,

Grows gradually louder as it nears,

Then fades as it moves away.

Someone died tonight.

Someone cried tonight.

Just another night in the city.

She takes a last drag on her Marlboro or Kool.

The cherry lights up a final time.

She exhales into the night,

And the smoke mingles with the steam coming up out of the sewer.

The woman drops the butt on the sidewalk,

Crushing it out with the red sole of her Louboutin's.

Crushed and discarded.

So is the cigarette.

She gives up and hails a cab.

"Where to?" he asks in a deep Slavic accent.

"Somewhere far from here," she replies,

Fighting back her tears,

For now.

"Somewhere far away."

<u>Stay Awake</u>

Can I stay awake for a few more minutes?

There are thoughts in my head I need to think;

I need to write them down before I forget.

I'm so tired.

My eyes are heavy,

I blink a little too long.

I remember and jerk awake.

Just a couple of minutes.

Tired,

My brain is shutting down.

Maybe I'll remember in the morning.

Maybe I'll dream about it,

And it will stay in my head.

Maybe I'll forget,

And maybe that will be better after all.

<u>Care</u>

Do you care?

No.

Do you care?

No.

What about you?

What about me?

Well, do you care?

Oh, no.

How about you over there, do you care?

I do not.

And you?

Nope.

Does anybody here care?

No.

Not at all?

No.

Crap. That's what I thought.

<u>Assimilate</u>

Assimilate. Assimilate?

Ruminate, Assassinate!

Take a pill

To cure your ills.

Take a pill,

Submit your will.

That's a good boy!

Welcome to my box of toys!

My universe, your world,

With all good little boys and girls.

Puppets, marionettes,

Aerialists without their safety nets.

Broken eggs, broken minds,

Just leave all that behind.

So, curtsy and bow

Do as I allow:

Where, when, and how.

You're my plaything now.

My pretty, pretty plaything.

Listen as I pull the string.

Song for Midnight (It Never Really Ends)

Soaring with angel and dragon,

Riding the waves of painted skies.

Breathing fire,

Blazing gold and crimson glory

In the mists above Valhalla's ships.

Plagued by sharks and spiders,

Rising,

Rising high above.

Heaven gained a siren demigod,

Transcendent over man,

Falling just shy of godhead.

Like Pandora's Box,

You were locked away,

Haunted by Death,

Burdened by Dumas,

Your mask of silver,

More precious than iron.

A prince who should be king,

Hidden away in the Valley of Shadows,

Shackled in your own Hell,

Bound by Shawna,

Filling your head with Pain,

Pain,

Pain,

And though the darkness held you close in a lover's embrace,

You never feared the dreaded reaper's blade.

You knew,

And you sang,

And you taught,

And you loved,

And you felt,

And the emotion was real.

The pain was real.

The love was real,

And we knew.

God,

How we knew!

You screamed and thrashed until Azrael granted mercy,

Released you from Shawna's chains.

Life could not hold you.

Death could not sway you,

Because in death you live.

We live,

Again.

You are unleashed from your attic prison!

You are free,

Free to spread your wings and fly to the heavens!

You are free to fly away and leave us behind,

In joy and in sorrow at our loss and your gain.

Heaven's gain!

Free from hurt and pain,

Fly away!

Fly away!

Look down sometime and see the flowers we planted for you,

Roses deep in the snow,

Crimson among the white,

Painted skies above,

Painted earth below,

Painted in our dreams,

Our hearts,

Our souls.

We long to soar with you with the holy angels,

To hear the magic once again.

The pain is gone.

The disease is gone.

You have found the cure.

You have found the answer,

And it never ends.

It never really ends.

Brotherman

Brotherman,

Brotherman,

You don't know how much I appreciate you.

We are broken,

Man.

We're broken,

But damn,

We've been put back together so many times.

Nuts,

Bolts,

Screws,

Duct tape,

Super glue,

More stitches than Frankenstein's monster.

The darkness has a call

Because the monsters walk in the sun.

The monsters walk right down the street in the sunlight,

With their heads held high

And smiles on their faces behind their sunglasses.

Man,

We're broken,

And we're ugly,

And we care,

And we love so freaking deeply,

And we pour ourselves out into what we do

Because we have to,

And that makes us freaking beautiful!

<u>The Fixer</u>

I dreamed a dream last night:

My Dad was in his wood shop.

As always,

He was building,

Creating,

Fixing.

He stepped over to the door of the shop and turned over a sign that
read,

"Fixer Open."

I blinked my eyes,

And all of a sudden,

There was this line,

A line of people,

A line of animals,

A line of toys,

A line of electronics,

A line of everything,

Everything…

Broken.

One by one,

The people,

The animals,

The toys,

The other things,

They entered,

One at a time.

My Dad bandaged,

He stitched,

He tinkered,

He hammered,

He drilled,

He cut,

He measured,

And he measured again

Because you always measure twice,

And one by one,

He fixed them all.

The line was long,

And my Dad was sweating.

I knew he wanted a beer and a cigarette,

But he didn't take a break;

He kept working,

He kept making,

He kept fixing.

Slowly,

Slowly,

The line shortened.

There were nuts and bolts and sawdust all around.

The sawdust hung in the air and covered my Dad's sweaty skin.

I could hear his raspy cough.

Finally,

The last patient was repaired,

Mended,

Fixed.

My Dad looked tired.

He was about to turn his sign to "Closed" when I called out for him
to wait.

I had been standing in the backyard the whole time,

Watching him work,

But then I ran over to him.

My Dad looked at me with tired,

But happy,

Eyes.

"Hey, son,"
He said.

"Dad,"

I started.

"What is it?"

He asked.

I threw my arms around him in a big hug.

He stiffened at first,

But then he put his arms around me.

"Nothing,"

I replied,

"You fixed me,"

I whispered,

Taking in the smell of sawdust,

Vitalis,

And wintergreen.

When I opened my eyes,

He was gone.

I was in my bed,

And my pillow was damp.

I was awake,

And he was gone again,

And I was wrong;

I wasn't fixed.

I wasn't mended.

I was still broken.

Just a Few Moments

Take me to a place where I can be alone,

For just a few moments at least.

You can drop me off,

Or you can sit in the shade and wait.

I probably won't be long.

When we get there,

I will just walk off by myself for a bit.

Maybe there'll be a trail that I can walk

And a wooden bridge over a small stream,

And I can sit on that bridge

And dangle my feet off the side.

I can listen to that brook for a few moments,

See what wisdom it can bestow upon me.

Perhaps there will be a butterfly,

Or a dragonfly,

Or a squirrel.

I like those.

I'll try not to be long.

I don't want you to worry.

I don't want it to get dark on us;

I know you don't like to drive in the dark.

Can we go now,

Please?

Can we please just go?

Okay,

Okay.

I'll get dressed.

I'll go to the bathroom and get ready.

I'll need just a few moments.

Maybe I'll just turn on the tub and give it a listen.

Maybe I'll sit on the edge of the tub and dangle my feet there.

Start the car,

I'm coming.

I'll be right there.

I have to get my walking shoes.

I just need a few moments.

<u>Let Go</u>

Buck up,

They say,

Only worry about the things you can control.

Live for

Today.

Don't grieve, you're only bringing us down.

They want me to forget/

They want me to forgive-myself.

They want me to forget.

They want me to let go,

But I won't let go.

I won't let go of you.

They think

I just sit around depressed.

They don't

Like my words.

They don't understand that my happy and my sad come from the
same place.

They want me to forget/

They want me to forgive-myself.

They want me to forget.

They want me to let go,

But I won't let go.

I won't let go of you.

They want me

To smile.

They don't care about what's going on inside.

Don't bring

Me down, man,

Just put on a mask when you're around us.

They want me to forget/

They want me to forgive-myself.

They want me to forget.

They want me to let go,

But I won't let go.

I won't let go of you.

My past

Is my life;

I draw on that for inspiration.

My future

Is not determined

But whether I'm happy or sad at this moment.

They want me to forget.

They want me to forgive-myself.

They want me to let go.

Not for me,

But for them,

But I won't let go.

I won't let go of you.

I won't let go.

Stormchoir

I hear them loud.

I hear them proud.

Thunder rolls across the sky like a drum,

Cymbals crash hear and there as the lightning flashes.

Rain drops pelt on metal roofs like a xylophone.

I hear coyotes howl in the distance,

A three-part harmony.

Somewhere,

A car alarm sounds,

Blaring into the night like a trumpet.

The wind whooshes past,

The flute and the clarinet,

And I sit here on my porch,

Strumming my six-string.

Nights like these,

The stormchoir comes alive,

Playing our greatest hits.

I Didn't Make It Out By Monday

I didn't make it out by Monday.

There were bills to pay that didn't get paid.

I looked out,

And there was a note in an envelope taped to the door.

I decided to leave it there.

There was food to be bought that didn't get bought.

I had saltines and Vienna sausage and a block of cheddar cheese that was fine once you cut the mold off the end.

I didn't have any fresh milk;

It was rurnt,

But I left it in the refrigerator anyway.

It needed to be poured down the drain,

But it didn't get poured down the drain.

There was trash that was overflowing and needed to be taken out that didn't get taken out.

The extra trash I had went into grocery store plastic bags that I reused from the last time I had gone out.

There were cable tv shows to be watched that didn't get watched
because the bills that need to be paid didn't get paid because I
didn't make it out by Monday.

The same with the shower,

And the electricity.

I didn't mind opening a window.

The screens were in,

And there was a nice breeze.

It turns cold at night,

So,

I shut the windows then.

It's okay because it feels like being outside without being outside.

When it rained the next day,

I set a bucket on the deck so I had water to wash with.

It felt good to be clean for a few minutes.

I looked in the cupboard and realized there were pills to take that
didn't get taken because I didn't make it out by Monday.

There is a refill somewhere.

It is dark here because the bill didn't get paid,

But I have candles.

I can read my Bible and my books and my papers by candlelight.

The flame's shadow makes eerie dance moves on the wall,

Swaying back and forth in the silence,

Because there is music to be played that cannot be played because
I didn't make it out by Monday.

I open the kitchen drawer.

There is a stapler,

And rubber bands,

And thumb tacks,

And AAA batteries,

And a pack of cinnamon gum,

And a tape measure,

And a bunch of envelopes with all my money.

There are more envelopes in more drawers,

And there are more in the closet,

And under the bed,

And some in a box under the sofa.

I look out the sliding glass window at the moon.

It tells me I could see better if I would just clean the glass,

But the glass didn't get cleaned.

Perhaps tomorrow.

I have papers to read and writings to write,

So,

Maybe not.

There are bills that need to get paid with the money in the
envelopes in the drawers,

But they probably won't get paid because I probably won't make it
out by Tuesday,

Either.

I sue the candle to look at the calendar.

Monday.

March 15.

Why does that seem wrong?

I pick up the newspaper off the kitchen table,

The one that came today,

I think.

Sunday.

June 13.

I thought the newspaper felt heavier.

I wondered why there were so many coupons to clip.

Sunday.

On a whim,

I flipped on the light switch by the refrigerator,

And the light turned on!

I raced to the sink and turned the faucet,

And hot water came out!

I looked at the newspaper again:

Sunday, June 13.

I hurried back to the front door,

Threw it open,

And snatched the envelope off it.

I pulled out the note,

Read it,

Read it again,

And walked back to the kitchen.

There was a door that needed to be closed that didn't get closed.

I dropped the note onto the table and picked up another newspaper
in the pile amongst the dirty plates.

March 15.

There,

In the left-hand corner of the front page,

I saw your name.

4C.

I turned out the kitchen light,

Extinguished the candle,

And sat for a long, long time,

Until it became Monday again.

There were bills to pay that wouldn't get paid

Because I wouldn't make it out by Monday.

<u>Drops of Rain, Surrender</u>

There is a time between the drops of rain

And the bouts of pain

When, for a moment,

I am, again, sane.

All these colors I see in my mind

Are like the rainbow in the sky

When the showers have stopped

And begin to dry up at the glimpse of the sun.

I can't close my eyes and end that sensation.

It blinds me,

This spectrum,

This miasma of reds and purples and blues and yellows.

It's like a prismatic cacophony;

I am overburdened by the sounds of color!

Hypersensitivity.

I can smell that gentle rain,

And I feel that pulsating throbbing in my head and hands.

I wish to lay magnets on my body,

Let the earth channel her forces through me,

Lounge in a hyperbolic chamber and decompress.

Hyperbolic hyperbole.

Let me just float on a sea of musical notes,

Something like Brahms,

Something like a lullaby,

Instead of this crashing,

Restless,

Devil went down to Georgia fiddle that's grinding along my spine!

I just want to lie face down,

Naked in the grass,

And let the rain pound my skin like acupuncture.

I just want to sleep under the stars and let the moon shine down on
me,

Feel gravity pull me down, down.

I just want this pain to go away,

But it's much more than just deep tissue,

Nothing a spa can ease.

Maybe I'll just wait for the flash flood to wash me down this track,

Down this creek,

To the river,

Out into the ocean and beyond.

Float,

Just float,

Allow myself to be carried away,

Let nature have her way and just…

Surrender.

<u>All Red</u>

My masculinity betrayed me.

I fell to my knees and screamed,

Cried,

Rose petals strewn across the glass-littered floor.

Thorns and shards dug into my knees,

My jeans ripped and frayed.

There was a face peering out from each silver surface,

Cold,

Bloody,

Horrid.

I stared at my red hands,

Red,

Knowing that the blood wasn't mine,

Red.

Not that blood.

Red.

Not that blood.

Those eyes burned into me,

Hundreds of little eyes everywhere,

Crying,

Pleading,

Wondering why.

Red.

Not a single one showed love.

In the end,

Red,

I think she was incapable.

That was fine for a while,

Red;

I had enough love for two.

I remember the roses,

Rose.

I remember the champagne,

Red.

The mirror?

Nothing but a blur,

A red blur.,

Hazy snapshots

Red.

Black heels,

Red.

A black dress,

Red.

They all turned red.

It all turned red.

I turned red.

She turned red.

Red.

It was all red.

Cream and Brown

See the mailbox, 805.

That is where I came alive.

Seahorses hanging on the brick

And shutter by the windows stick.

Chain-linked fence with double-gate,

Two-car driveway, concrete paved.

Flower beds on either side.

This is where I came alive.

Once white and blue,

Now cream and brown.

Front yard with a wishing well.

White swing where we'd sit a spell.

My Dad and I, we'd toss a ball

Into a pail. I was so small.

Crepe myrtles and two giant pines,

A weeping willow, ivy vines.

Spent many hours raking straw

And picking cones up off the lawn.

Cream and brown.

In the backyard I'd shoot hoops

Or catch a ball thrown on the stoop.

A 4-foot pool in which we swam.

We always said yes sir and ma'am.

A fig tree full of sticky figs,

Watch for holes the dogs would dig.

So many, many hours spent;

I never knew just what it meant.

Cream and brown.

The shop where Dad would cut and build

Bird house, toy boxes; He was skilled.

He could make or fix most anything.

To go back, I'd give everything.

It's been 10 years I've been away.

I miss it each and every day.

Just three returns, and all sad times.

I hate I've had to say goodbye,

And it pains me day by day.

I miss the place that my head laid,

But there is nothing left but ghosts.

Still, it's the place I miss the most.

One day, perhaps, I'll be back home,

Back to where I used to roam

And feel those memories once again

At the place we'd paint and stain

Cream and brown.

Cream and brown.

Pendulum

The pendulum swings,

Again, and again,

Slowly,

Mockingly,

Glinting silver murder by the light of a thousand candles.

I am not bound,

Not physically,

But I cannot move.

Enchanted,

Bewitched,

Entranced by the swaying rhythm of impending doom,

As the pendulum lowers,

Closer,

Closer,

Close…

<u>Lace Over Ink</u>

Lace over ink,

It makes me think,

And I want to know…

What's on that skin?

What can I do to be let in?

Lace over in,

I'm starting to sink,

And I need to know…

What is in her world?

What is the meaning behind those swirls?

Black lace and skin,

I don't know where to begin,

But I need to touch…

What will she say?

Would she dare to drive me away?

White lace and flesh,

She and I, enmeshed,

I don't know where it will end...

I think I've been enslaved,

But I go happily, happily, happily to my grave.

<u>Bones of Saints</u>

I bought a bone of one St. Paul.

I have it in a case down the hall.

It's part of a finger, knuckle bone,

But I did not want it to be alone,

So, I found a bone of St. Stephen.

Two bones made it even.

This one, I think, was a little toe.

I wrapped it with a light blue bow,

But then I was offered another one:

A piece of the clavicle of Adomnan.

He was from the land of Scot.

I bought it in a lot

That also had bones from Baralus,

Also known as St. Romanus,

And a bone from one St. Edith Stein,

Who had died on August 9.

I was set to buy quite a few more

Until a knock fell on my door.

There stood an aged, withered man

Who promptly told me I'd been had.

He knew the one who'd sold the bones,

Said I should leave that one alone,

Quickly I was told and shown

That what I'd bought were chicken bones!

They were not really even old.

Stupidly I'd traded gold.

I asked the man how he had known.

He shook his head, let out a moan

And said his wife had left him lone

So many, many years ago

When he had bought similar bones.

He had seen the same ads that I'd seen

And knew he had to intervene.

He offered gold to buy them back;

I knew he must have been a hack

Trying to trick me from my bones.

I sent him out with quite a groan

And laughed, as I was not a tool

And would not be taken for a fool.

Chicken bones? No, I think not.

Bones of saints are what I'd bought!

I will keep them very, very neat,

But I wonder why they smell of chicken meat?

<u>Yeller</u>

Rockefeller,

Longfeller,

Bob Feller,

I'm a yeller,

Coward.

See the streak down this here back?

I'm a runner,

Not a gunner,

Just a funner,

Comedian.

Want to hear a knock-knock joke?

Knock knock?

Who's there?

Yeller.

Yeller who?

Yeller in his underwear,

That's who!

Who?

Who?

There's that damned owl again.

He's a'testin' me,

With his beak

And them eyes,

And that twirly head crap,

Like somethin' outta that Exorcist,

Linda Blair freaky deaky stuff.

Uh uh,

I'm a runnin'.

See?

That's what they calls a pattern,

My m.o.

I'm afraid of so many things:

Snakes, spiders, scorpions,

Cats, bats, rats,

Talkin' horses,

Like Mr. Ed,

Ice cream men,

Clowns,

Little fish bitin' at your toes,

Black-eyed peas.

Those things look like they're watchin' you.

That's just a few of 'em.

Don't get me started.

Maybe you should just go.

Can you please just go,

Okay?

I think I've said enough,

And I'm whooped.

Gonna have a nice cold glass of sweet tea.

I'd ask you to join me,

But you're kinda scarin' me right now.

You gotta go.

Dirty Dishes

Dirty dishes in the sink,

Filled up to the brink,

And I think,

I think,

That I don't care.

There are cobwebs in the corners

And dust bunnies around the borders.

This place,

With its towers of books and magazines and music CDs,

Looks like hoarders,

And I think,

I think,

I don't care.

In the fridge is expired milk

And something red that's growing silk,

And I think…

I need to dust,

I need to sweep,

I need to mop,

I need to wash clothes,

I need to buy detergent to wash clothes,

I need to put books back on their shelves,

I need to change out the batteries in the television remote,

I need to change out the batteries in the smoke detector,

And I really need to take a shower.

The grass has grown up to the windows.

There are leaves to rake and branches to pick up from the storm

And gutters to clean

And a roof to mend

And windows to wash,

And,

And,

And,

It's too much.

Maybe I'll just move.

Maybe I'll just burn it down,

Collect the insurance,

And move to a little cabin somewhere in the woods,

Near a lake or a stream,

And I can bathe outside when I want,

But someplace close enough so I can get Clorox and Murphy's Oil,

And Pop Tarts.

The rest can go to hell.

The cobwebs and the dust bunnies can have it all.

<u>Sorting Out My Mystery</u>

Who am I,

And where do I belong?

I don't think I've ever really known.

I'm learning,

Evolving,

Forgetting,

Reflecting on the past,

Considering what the future could entail.

I've always thought that you didn't know me.

Now I know I didn't myself,

But you knew that all along.

My insanity has always been my mystery,

But I'm not insane at all,

And you knew that, too.

I'm a pretender.

I wish to be insane so that I can be more interesting,

Eclectic.

In truth,

I am quite boring,

And that is what I try to hide.

I am a liar,

And I only want you to like me.

I want your love and your attention,

And I don't really know why.

I'm an uninteresting,

Procrastinating,

Liar,

And I seek validation that I don't really need.

I guess it's not such a mystery after all.

<u>Lonely Paradise</u>

It's so beautiful here in my garden,

My paradise.

I have flowers and trees

And puppies and bees

Green grass, blue skies,

Where nothing dies.

I have the music of angels,

And I sing, and I sing!

I have a library of the greatest books:

Shakespeare, Poe, Hawthorne, King,

Meltzer, Homer…everything!

I have walls of the greatest art:

Van Gogh, Van Gogh, Van Gogh.

Munch, Monet, Da Vinci, Dali,

Sculptures of the Pieta, David, DeMilo.

I have it all!

Everything I've ever wanted to see,

Read,

Hear.

Everything I've ever wanted.

Wonders and treasures and beauty everywhere I look,

But, I haven't found you.

I search the trees and the streams and behind the statues,

And I know you have to be hiding,

Silly goose!

Where are you?

I look, and I search, and I call your name.

Where are you?

I can't find you,

But you have to be here!

All this beauty,

This Heaven,

This lonely paradise!

You have to be here,

Otherwise,

It is not a paradise,

It is a lonely,

Lonely hell.

Good and Evil

What if we hadn't taken that bite?

What if we'd chosen to remain innocent?

That if we had chosen to believe?

What if we had remained obedient?

What if we didn't know good and evil?

What if the veil wasn't lifted from our eyes?

What if we didn't know good and evil?

What if we didn't believe the lies?

What if we had believed in the promise?

What if we had remained content?

What if we had turned from temptation?

What if we would just relent?

What if we didn't know good and evil?

What if the veil wasn't lifted from our eyes?

What if we didn't know good and evil?

What if we didn't believe the lies?

What if we could go back?

What if we could change the past?

What if we could turn to love?

What if we could make it last?

What if we didn't know good and evil?

What if the veil wasn't lifted from our eyes?

What if we didn't know good and evil?

What if we believed the promises instead of the lies?

Time, Could You Please Hold On?

Time,

Could you please hold on a minute?

Stop your ticking for a while.

I need a few seconds,

A few minutes.

I need another year or two.

I need to spend more time with my wife and kids.

There are more places I want to visit,

More art I want to see,

More music I want to listen to,

More books I want to read.

I have so many ideas in my head,

Poetry,

Stories,

Songs to write.

I have to get this all down.

Who is going to cut the grass?

Who is going to wheel the trash up the driveway?

Who is going to shovel the snow?

Who is going to be the remote-control lord?

You see,

Time?

I have so much to do.

Can you please slow down?

Can't you please just stop?

There you go again,

Counting down another minute!

Stop it!

I have grandkids to meet!

Great grandkids to me!

Great-great grandkids I want to meet!

I need to go visit my parents' graves.

I want to visit my old house,

See my old bedroom.

I want…

I need…

You don't care.

I'm going to unplug you,

Clock!

I'm going to take out your batteries!

I'm going to rest you,

Wind the time back!

That will show you!

You'd better listen!

I mean it!

I mean it.

Please,

Can you please just give me a little more,

Time?

Avoid the Flood

You failed to listen,

Two by two,

Many warnings

Issued you.

The end is near,

The time is nigh.

The ocean waters

Rising high.

You should have listened

When you had your chance.

Now, you're all alone.

Avoid the flood,

It's raining blood,

And there's nowhere,

My Guardian Anger

Nowhere to run.

Avoid the tide

That's on all sides,

And there's nowhere,

Nowhere to hide.

Stars are falling,

Oceans boil.

There are poisons in the soil.

The end is here,

The signs are there,

Bodies floating everywhere.

You should have listened

When you had your chance.

Now, you're all alone.

Avoid the flood,

It's raining blood,

And there's nowhere,

Nowhere to run.

Avoid the tide

That's on all sides,

And there's nowhere,

Nowhere to hide.

The evil that men do,

The hate, the scorn,

The sins are all accounted for.

You should have listened.

Avoid the flood,

It's raining blood,

And there's nowhere,

Nowhere to run.

Avoid the tide

That's on all sides,

And there's nowhere,

Nowhere to hide.

There's nowhere,

Nowhere to hide.

<u>Eyes Crying</u>

Eyes crying,

I'm trying

To breathe,

To keep from dying.

It seems

My world is shattered.

The world spins on,

But it doesn't matter

When the hope is gone.

Where's my book,

The Word?

Where to look?

Luke, John, Psalms, Proverbs?

What will God say

When He knows I want to give me life away?

He knows,

That's why He has stayed my hand

And throws me to the floor. I no longer stand;

I kneel and pray.

I know I need my Lord this day,

And I sit silent,

And I listen,

My thoughts no longer violent.

I'm forgiven,

And my tears are dried.

I believe,

And my faith is revived.

I receive

His love,

His blessings,

From above.

I will keep pressing

On,

More work to do.

I know that He's not through with me.

I know that I'm not through,

And I am free.

<u>Pretty Hate You</u>

Here I am.

Here are you.

Pretty hate me.

Pretty hate you.

Pretty lips.

Pretty eyes.

Pretty hate your

Cheap disguise.

Pretty skin.

Pretty hair.

Pretty hate you

Everywhere.

Here I am.

Pretty hate me.

Pretty fingers.

Pretty toes.

Pretty hate you.

Everyone knows.

Pretty smile.

Pretty ears.

Pretty hate you

Whenever you're near.

Here you are.

Pretty hate you.

Pretty tongue.

Pretty voice.

Pretty hate you

And your noise.

Pretty chin.

Pretty teeth.

Pretty hate

You're personality.

Pretty.

Pretty.

Pretty.

Pretty.

Hate.

Hate.

Hate.

Hate.

Everything about you is pretty.

Everything about you is perfect.

I have everything about you.

I hate you.

I hate me for loving you.

I hate you for hating me.

I hate me for hating you.

I hate you for loving me.

Pretty hate you.

Pretty hate me.

Let's go get a coffee so I can stare at you for a bit.

I hate how pretty you are.

Pretty hate me.

<u>Can't Tell You Why</u>

I can't tell you why

Good people up and die.

It's strange.

It's a hard thing to embrace.

I can't tell you why

Sometimes I lie.

I never mean to,

But that's also a lie.

I can't tell you why

I often sit and cry.

I could,

But you don't have that much time.

So many things I can't tell you

Or won't tell you.

Maybe if you asked,

Maybe if you really wanted to know,

Maybe if I trusted you enough,

But I don't,

And I can't tell you why.

There's just something there,

Something in your eyes,

Something that isn't quite right,

And maybe I should've known,

Maybe before I let you in,

Maybe before I let it begin.

I should've known,

But I don't know why.

Maybe what's in your eyes is just my reflection.

Maybe that's what's wrong.

I'm not sure that I know much of anything,

And sometimes that's better.

Sometimes it's better if I don't know,

But I can't tell you why.

<u>Stolen</u>

Stolen,

Overloaded,

Lost chances,

Lost profits,

Lost prophets,

Lost cause.

Stolen

Happiness,

Purity,

Independence,

Dependent and hurting,

Struggling,

Pains,

Pains,

Pains,

Ills,

Ill wills,

Thoughts,

Impure thoughts,

Nightmares.

Why weren't these stolen?

Come back!

Come back,

You forgot something!

You forgot these!

Stolen,

Took away the dreams,

The promises,

The prosperity,

The love,

The victory.

I think you just came in and dropped off your crap.

It's not a trade.

It's not a fair deal.

It's not a new deal.

It's an old, old deal.

Take your crap back,

And give me back my crap you've stolen.

You've stolen,

Wretched thief!

You've stolen…

Everything.

You've stolen everything

<u>A Dream Within a Dream Within a Dream</u>

Running, Falling!

Wake up!

I jerk my eyes open,

And the thing in the corner shifts,

Moves a step towards my bed.

I pull the covers up and close my eyes again;

I see black and white squares,

Rainbow lights passing through my vision.

It's a haze.

It's a blur.

It's not real.

It's not real!

I open my eyes again.

It's black,

And I can't see,

But I remember the cover over my head.

I pull it slowly,

Carefully down to my nose.

The thing is still there,

Dark hand upon the bedpost at the foot of the bed.

I can hear its raspy wheeze.

I throw one of the pillows at the shape,

But the pillow just passes through it,

Bounces off my dresser,

Rattling the mirror,

Knocking my Magic 8-ball to the floor.

It rolls towards me on the cold, wooden floor,

And I pick it up.

"Will that thing get me tonight?"

I ask in a whisper,

As I shake up the 8-ball while keeping my eyes on the specter.

I take a quick glance down at the screen,

Watch the tetrahedron in the blue liquid.

"Concentrate and ask again,"

Is its reply.

I do as the 8-ball commands,

Closing my eyes and shaking the orb.

When I open my eyes,

The thing is a foot closer.

"Better not to tell you now,"

The 8-ball reads.

I close my eyes a third time,

Shaking the 8-ball vigorously.

My eyes are affixed to the black and white sphere.

The liquid sloshes inside,

And I can feel a bony hand caress my throat.

"My sources say no,"

The 8-ball displays.

I steel myself and look up.

The dark, ghostly figure has dissolved into the shadows.

I take a large breatg and exhale slowly.

Once more,

I look down at the Magic 8-Ball.

My lips quiver.

"Ask again later,"

It tells me.

<u>Gravity</u>

I saw you,

And I fell.

I was falling,

I was falling down.

Caught your smell,

What the hell,

And I fell.

I was falling

Down,

Down,

Down.

Down,

Down,

Down.

Didn't know

What to do,

I was falling,

I was falling for you.

Couldn't lie,

Wouldn't cry,

Can't deny

That I'm falling

Down,

Down,

Down.

Down,

Down,

Down.

Gravity,

It's holding me,

Holding me,

Holding me down.

I'm being pulled,

Being fooled,

Being schooled

By this gravity.

I was scared,

You wouldn't care,

You were walking,

You were walking away.

Couldn't spare,

Wouldn't dare,

Saw you walking,

I was falling

Down,

Down,

Down.

Down,

Down,

Down.

Lost my voice,

Lost my choice,

My Guardian Anger

I had fallen,

I had fallen down.

When you winked,

Couldn't blink,

I kept falling,

Kept on falling

Down,

Down,

Down.

Down,

Down,

Down.

Gravity,

It's holding me,

Holding me,

Holding me down.

I'm being pulled,

Being fooled,

Being schooled

By this gravity.

Down,

Down,

Down.

Down,

Down,

Down.

Down,

Down,

Down.

Down,

Down,

Down.

Down.

Gravity,

It's holding me,

Holding me,

Holding me down.

I'm being pulled,

Being fooled,

Being schooled

By this gravity.

<u>Staring Down the Barrel</u>

Sometimes, life has a way

Of kicking you when you're down.

You wear your heart upon your sleeve,

Get treated like a fool or clown.

All your friends and family,

The ones supposed to have your back,

The first ones that take the long, cold knife

And drive it in your back.

So, you pull away

And leave the world behind,

But you find that the solitude

Is playing games with your mind.

Staring down the barrel,

Not caring, wild and feral.

Tired of a life so sterile.

Staring down the barrel.

When you feel like you've had enough,

You gotta take back control.

If you don't, you will find yourself

Lying in a six-foot hole.

I know you've got these crazy thoughts

Spinning inside your brain.

Take a moment, gotta take a breath

Before you let it drive you insane.

So, you pull away

And leave the world behind,

But you find that the solitude

Is playing games with your mind.

Staring down the barrel,

Not caring, wild and feral.

Tired of a life so sterile.

Staring down the barrel.

Get out!

Get loose!

Just shout!

Don't lose!

Staring down the barrel,

Not caring, wild and feral.

Tired of a life so sterile.

Staring down the barrel.

<u>Coughing</u>

Coughing?

Why you coughing so much?

Why you wheezing?

Did you smoke too much?

Did you smoke too long?

Did the toxins get down into your lungs,

Down, down,

Into the bronchioles?

Is it asthma?

Is it bronchitis?

Is it pneumonia?

Is it cancer?

I'll toast you.

You look like you need a toast.

You deserve to be honored.

You're a good person.

You're pretty cool.

Here's to you!

You want a drink?

Maybe it'll wash out that smoke,

Wash down that smoke.

Maybe it'll dilute it.

Man,

That cough is bad!

Are you bringing anything up?

You might want to see a doctor,

A specialist,

A pulmonologist.

Dude,

There's a shaman just outside of town.

No,

Not a witch doctor.

Holistic,

Man.

Natural,

Herbal.

Hey,

Here's your drink.

Wash it on down,

Down,

Down.

Yeah,

It's calming you already.

Has anybody ever told you that you sound like Eartha Kitt?

Sorry,

I mean no offense.

She was cool,

Too;

Catwoman.

Dude,

You okay?

Keep coughing.

Yeah,

Keep coughing.

Wow,

Is that blood?

I think you need to see somebody.

Yeah,

You might want to see somebody soon.

<u>Mis Kerzu</u>

The earth is farthest from the sun this time of year.

Days are shorter,

Nights come early,

Linger longer.

Cold days,

Colder nights,

With only the warmth of a fire,

Or another close body,

To dispel the chill and death.

The nights are clearer,

The stars are brighter,

And the doors to Heaven and Hell are open wide.

Angels and devils walk and prowl,

With no one the wiser.

We are passing from one to the next,

The old to the new,

And the Yule is not the only thing to burn away.

Ashes of dreams,

Ashes of memories.

It is mis kerzu,

The very black month,

And when the world should rejoice and welcome peace,

The darkness breaks the windows,

Kicks down doors,

Letting the bitterness in,

And regret claims another victim.

Regret settles in,

With a mug of hot chocolate,

A paper,

And its slippers,

And it will sit and stay for a long,

Long time.

<u>Drowning in Sin</u>

I've seen you time and time again

Returning to your bottle.

You fight a battle you can't win,

Speeding at full throttle.

The pain and rage you hold inside,

Too scared to talk about it.

No one to trust who's on your side,

And all you do is doubt.

You live your life

In the bottom of a poisoned lie.

You can't deny

That you're hanging by a thread this time.

Drowning in sin,

All it takes is that one drink.

Drowning in sin,

It takes away the pain, that's what you think.

Drowning in sin,

It's the only friend that's been there for you.

Drowning in sin,

It's a battle that you know you're gonna lose.

You lost your wife, you lost your kids

To this disease.

You lost your job, you cannot work,

Only you hold the keys.

You have to fight, you have to want

To get any better.

Put down that drink and stop to think,

No scarlet letters.

You live your life

In the bottom of a poisoned lie.

You can't deny

That you're hanging by a thread this time.

Drowning in sin,

All it takes is that one drink.

Drowning in sin,

It takes away the pain, that's what you think.

Drowning in sin,

It's the only friend that's been there for you.

Drowning in sin,

It's a battle that you know you're gonna lose.

You live your life

In the bottom of a poisoned lie.

You can't deny

That you're hanging by a thread this time.

Drowning in sin,

All it takes is that one drink.

Drowning in sin,

It takes away the pain, that's what you think.

Drowning in sin,

It's the only friend that's been there for you.

Drowning in sin,

It's a battle that you can't afford to lose.

<u>Gardens and Graves</u>

Between the gardens and graves,

Only few know their names.

How many were saved?

How many were blamed?

Live flowers here,

Dead flowers there,

But in the winters,

Both are bare,

And the faces fade from memory,

And the names fade on the stones,

And the flowers wilt and the petals fall,

And the bushes and the stones are all that remain.

<u>Upon the Wind</u>

Words stream out of my mouth

Before I can stop them,

And they float away upon the wind.

Upon the wind.

I don't know if you heard,

And I don't know where they went,

Out there upon the wind.

Upon the wind.

Everything that's bad passes on

Upon the wind.

Everything good passes on

Upon the wind.

Everything passes.

I could say I'm sorry,

But those words would just rise, too,

Rise and float upon the wind.

Upon the wind.

All the "I love yous,"

All of our prayers,

They float to Heaven upon the wind.

Upon the wind.

Everything that's bad passes on

Upon the wind.

Everything good passes on

Upon the wind.

Everything passes.

All the curses,

All the laughs and tears,

All the seconds, minutes, years,

Upon the wind.

Everything that's bad passes on

Upon the wind.

Everything good passes on

Upon the wind.

Everything passes,

Everything passes,

Everything passes on

Upon the wind.

<u>Have to Be Right</u>

I'm right!

Shut up!

I'm right!

I will be right!

I have to be right,

And I will talk over you,

I will yell over you,

I will scream over you,

So, even if I'm not right,

I will be right

Because no one will be able to hear you,

And it doesn't matter that I come off as an ass,

It doesn't matter what they think of me,

It doesn't matter what you think of me,

You will be wrong,

And I will be right.

Just shut your mouth now so I don't have to scream,

But I will if I have to

Because I am right,

And I have to be right,

And you have to be wrong.

<u>Stone Eyes</u>

Stone eyes stare down at me,

Stone eyes with tears at their corners.

Stone eyes stand guard,

Keeping the world at bay,

Away.

Stone wings lay folded against a stone back;

No need to fly just now.

Stone arms hang down,

With stone hands holding a stone sword,

The point of which touches the stone pedestal upon which it
stands.

All around me,

Stones and grass,

Grass and stones.

I am the only living person in this field,

Yet,

I feel more dead than those already in the ground.

I feel hard like these stones.

Perhaps I will find my own pedestal,

And I will stand and watch,

Protect,

Regard.

I won't have wings,

But there is no need for me to fly.

I won't have a sword,

But there is nothing right now to fight.

I am just a stone.

Life,

And death,

Have hardened me.

I am no stranger here.

I am home.

I Am Illuminati

I am Illuminati,

And you want to know the answers,

The answers that I know.

There's an eye,

And there's an eye,

And there's an I,

But you already know this.

You already know the answers.

You already know what I know,

But you can't see,

Won't see.

It is all around you:

Knowledge,

Wisdom,

Power,

God,

But you're afraid.

Reach out for it,

Grab it,

Take hold of it,

Fill yourself up with it,

Drink it up,

Et it up,

Breathe it in!

Unplug yourself from your tech and plug yourself into the world.

It's up.

It's down.

It's left.

It's right.

It's inside and outside.

I sit beneath this tree,

Like Sir Isaac,

And I watch you fumbling around,

Like a child with a blindfold on.

"Where's my hotspot?"

"Why can't I get signal?"

"Why is my Bluetooth not working?"

You're lost and you're scared.

Ignorance is scary.

You reach out for me,

But I've already climbed up the tree.

Come on!

You try to climb,

But I go higher and higher,

And you need a hand to hold your phone.

You want to learn?

You want to know?

Keep reaching.

Keep climbing.

You don't have to be ignorant.

You are choosing to be ignorant.

You don't have to be anymore.

The answers you seek are here.

Reach,

Baby.

Keep reaching.

I'm waiting.

Make the effort,

And I'll take your hand and pull you up.

<u>Grandude</u>

Grandude,

You've got a lot of gray in your hair,

Grandude.

Grandude,

I think you fell asleep in your chair,

Grandude.

Grandude,

You've told that joke a million times,

Grandude.

Grandude,

You can't lemonade with a lime,

Grandude.

Grandude.

Grandude.

Grandude.

Grandude.

Grandude,

I love it when we go to your house,

Grandude.

Grandude,

You've got a really cute, white little mouse,

Grandude.

Grandude,

Can you take us through the woods for a walk,

Grandude?

Grandude,

We love to sit on logs and just talk,

Grandude.

Grandude.

Grandude.

Grandude.

Grandude.

Grandude,

Can we sleep over tonight,

Grandude?

Grandude,

Tell us scary tales to give us a fright,

Grandude.

Grandude,

Maybe make hot chocolate with milk,

Grandude.

Grandude,

Race you up and over the hill,

Grandude.

Grandude.

Grandude.

Grandude.

Grandude.

We love you,

Grandude.

Spin Out

Spin out,

Spiraling down,

Out of control.

Lights out,

Falling blind,

Into the unknown.

Too fast,

Take the wheel,

Pumping brakes.

Head dizzy,

Pulse race,

Body shakes.

Spin out,

Out of control.

Spin out,

Out of control.

Spin out,

Out of control.

Spin out,

Out of control.

Lost way,

Missed my mark,

Crying shame.

Snared in

To a trap,

I'm to blame.

Another hit,

Another drink

Is all it took.

Turned away,

Lead astray,

Should've turned to the Book.

Spin out,

Out of control.

Spin out,

Out of control.

Spin out,

Out of control.

Spin out,

Out of control.

Turn back, turn back, turn back, turn back, turn back.

Turn back, turn back, turn back, turn back, turn back.

Turn back, turn back, turn back, turn back, turn back.

Turn back, turn back, turn back, turn back, turn back.

Spin out,

Out of control.

Spin out,

Out of control.

Spin out,

Out of control.

Spin out,

Out of control.

Spin out,

Out of control.

Spin out,

Out of control.

Spin out,

Out of control.

Spin out,

Out of control.

Spin out,

Out of control.

<u>Pile of Bones</u>

I wake in the morning,

Put all my bones back in place,

Tie the tendons and muscles to their spots,

And zip myself up in my flesh suit.

It used to take a couple of hours,

But it takes me no time at all now.

I pick a face from the rack by the closet,

Slap it on,

Grab a hair piece,

Snap it in place.

All done,

I take a moment to look in the mirror,

Making sure I look just right,

Or as right as I can.

Amazing how no one notices.

I look just how everyone expects me to look,

How they expect me to be:

Happy,

Perfect,

Human.

It will be a long day,

As always.

I can't wait to get back home and drop back into my pile of bones.

<u>Bitter Cold</u>

November,

And it's bitter cold.

I'm feeling less than bold

As I shiver.

It's not all from the breeze;

It's everything I feel and see.

Fallen leaves,

With their browns and reds

Conjure up images of the dead,

And the birds that fail to veer

Away from the bay window,

I fear,

Are lying in the grass below.

I'd bury them,

But I know

There will be more,

Outside the window,

Outside the door,

And my soul mourns for them.

I put seed in the feeder,

Hang it on a branch in the maple tree,

Away from the house,

Away from the windows,

But in a place where I can watch from my couch,

The cardinals,

The blue jays,

The robins,

The doves,

And others I do not know,

And I am too lazy to research.

The rain is falling now,

Gently upon the roof.

I can hear it,

And I can feel it in my broken bones.

Tonight,

It will turn to ice,

Or maybe snow.

Maybe there'll be sledding.

Maybe there'll be snowball fights.

There will definitely be coffee and hot chocolate.

I may step out onto the porch,

If I dare to brave the chill,

And the ill will,

And I will hear the bells,

And the car horns honking,

And the ambulance sirens,

And the coyotes yipping nearby.

I hear another thunk as something hits the window.

I look,

Quickly,

But it has flown away,

Thank God.

Fly away,

Fly away!

Migrate if you can!

Go South,

To the warmth.

It's cold.

So cold,

So cold.

Maybe I should migrate, too.

<u>Cockroaches</u>

I turn on the light,

And you're there.

I leave my food on the counter,

And you're there.

You're crawling on the floor,

Crawling on the walls,

Inside the walls,

In the closets,

Up in the attic,

And you have no freaking purpose in my life!

I spray,

And I stomp,

And I flush,

And you just keep coming back!

My Guardian Anger

I don't want to kill;

I'm not like that,

But you're an invader,

And this is war!

Take no prisoners!

You're always here,

Eavesdropping,

Spying,

Waiting.

You little parasites!

I put my food away,

And you still linger to see what I'm going to do.

You're dirty and filthy,

And I want you out!

Get out!

Leave me alone!

Go crawl and feed and eavesdrop somewhere else.

You're not welcome here.

Just go next door.

I hear they have better food.

<u>Sire Schemes</u>

I sire schemes

And plots and dreams

With gladness

And madness

And sadness.

I thank you

And you

And you all.

Your loyalty,

Your brutality,

Is known to me.

I welcome your words

And your gifts of birds

And books

And surly looks.

Do you think that I don't hear

What you say when you think I'm not near?

Do you think that I don't see

The beads of sweat in your treachery?

What I know is real,

And this I feel

Is to be my undoing

From your perpetual wooing.

I am not your consort,

Not your escort!

I am a king,

A regal being,

And I will be treated as such!

Can I ask that much?

I demand it to be so,

And what you fail to know

Is that I get what I demand

From air and sea and land.

Be gone, as I walk these halls!

I don't want to hear your screams in these walls!

Leave me alone

With my soul and my bones.

I have much more plotting to do,

So many dreams and schemes to put my mind through,

And it is my cross to bear alone

As I falter towards my dusty throne.,

Leave the jackets at the door.

I won't need them anymore,

But thank you,

Thank you.

That will be all.

As you were.

<u>Bite My Tongue</u>

Ooh,

I've got something to say,

But there's no way

It will keep the peace.

Ooh,

I better hide away,

I better run away

Before I spread your disease.

I'm gonna bite my tongue

And watch it bleed.

Bite my tongue

'Til I can't see.

Bite my tongue,

Or I'll regret.

Bite my tongue,

But I won't forget.

Ooh,

I've been holding inside.

I know you've lied,

But I cannot speak.

Ooh,

For all our sakes,

This pain I'll take,

But I'm feeling weak.

I'm gonna bite my tongue

And watch it bleed.

Bite my tongue

'Til I can't see.

Bite my tongue,

Or I'll regret.

Bite my tongue,

But I won't forget.

Ooh,

You're not worth my spit.

I'll walk away and quit.

This will get us nowhere.

Ooh,

You will never change.

Get out of my range

Before I start to care.

I'm gonna bite my tongue

And watch it bleed.

Bite my tongue

'Til I can't see.

Bite my tongue,

Or I'll regret.

Bite my tongue,

But I won't forget.

No, I won't forget.

No, I won't forget.

No, I will never forget.

My Bones

My body was left on the ground to rot,

For the wild animals to feed upon,

For the earth to be fertilized.

I watched in rage and misery

As my bones were picked clean.

There was nothing I could do to stop the assault.

Helpless.

I couldn't shew away the flies and the vultures and the coyotes,

But I took slight comfort in knowing they would not go hungry.

Nothing but bones,

Nothing but my bones left.

I tried,

And I tried hard,

To pick them up,

Buy my hands went right through them.

I wanted to dig in the soil and bury my bones,

To put what was left of me to rest.

I strained my soul as much as I could until it felt like I would be
ripped in two.

My hope was that somehow,

Someone would find my bones,

Maybe report them to someone else,

And I could be interred somewhere in a potter's field.

Anywhere but here,

But no one has come.

No one.

My bones still wait.

I still wait for my peace.

<u>Under the Moon</u>

Under the moon,

You're under my skin.

I don't know where to begin.

Radiance,

And the fire in your touch;

I feel I've said and done too much.

It's too soon to drive you away;

We'll save that for some other day.,

But I will cherish these precious minutes

And the feel of the earth beneath us,

The smells, and your hair,

Your eyes, and everywhere

I touch feels like magic.

Everything else in the world, they can have it

As long as I have this,

This moment,

And your kiss.

One fleeting moment of bliss,

And I would be remiss

If I didn't close my eyes

And drink it all in as time slips by.

Under the moon,

This will be over soon,

But there will never,

Ever be a day

When I don't remember you and I this way.

I can't even think about what tomorrow has in store.

Under the moon,

Right now,

Is all I'll ever ask for.

<u>Brothers</u>

This is for a brother who was gone too soon.

This is for a brother that I truly knew

Like the back of my hands,

Counting down the sands.

This is for a brother with an angel's voice.

This is for a brother, and we made a choice

To be more than a band,

Here, we're counting down the sands.

We were four,

And now we're two.

Hate to watch the evening news

And have to say goodbye.

Brothers, you made me cry.

This is for a brother with a heart of gold.

This is for a brother, nothing fills the hole

Deep within my heart,

Fifty years apart.

This is for a brother with a smile so wide.

This is for a brother, I could never hide

Oh, the way I feel.

What we had was real.

We were four,

And now we're two.

Hate to watch the evening news

And have to say goodbye.

Brothers, you made me cry.

We were four,

And now we're two.

Hate to watch the evening news

And have to say goodbye.

Brothers, you made me cry.

We were four,

And now we're two.

Hate to watch the evening news

And have to say goodbye.

Brothers, you made me smile.

Brothers, you made me smile.

Brothers, you made me smile.

<u>Pen Tops</u>

You like to take the tops off ink pens,

And you hide them.

You know that pisses me off so much!

How can you do that?

It's just a waste of ink,

And it's hard to find a good pen,

One that writes just right,

Smooth,

Without any gaps when you write,

Without any little ink booger globs,

Without any ink that smears.

Damnit,

Why do you do that?

If I have a click pen,

You click it and leave it open.

If I have a fountain pen,

You will turn it so the pen nib is sticking out,

And you leave it that way!

Why? Why? Why?

You know how crazy that drives me!

Yes,

You do;

That's why you do it!

You want me to be crazy,

But don't you know I already am!

You don't try to crazy up a crazy person!

Leave my pens alone!

You don't even like to write.

Don't make me take my pens and lock them up.

I'll do it!

I swear I'll do it!

You know I will.

You know I will.

These are good pens.

<u>Dirty Hands</u>

Dirty hands,

And callouses;

I've been digging all day,

I've been shoveling all day.

I've been scraping and grinding and burning.

There's mud and blood under my nails.

Gloves are useless,

I wear through them,

Torn, frayed, holes burnt.

It's okay,

It's fine.

I like the dirt on my hands.

I like the cuts and the scratches,

And the blood.

It's hard,

But it's soothing.

I forget the crap that's going on around me,

And when I'm done,

Though I'm never truly done,

I jump in the hot shower,

Get lathered up,

Rub my hands together,

Scratch my nails into my palms to get them clean,

Run my fingers through my hair and across my scalp,

Let the room get steamy,

Write my words of love and thanks on the shower glass,

And relish the near-scalding water rolling off my head and down my back.

It washes it all away,

Clears my head and heart.

Tomorrow is another day,

And I will dirty my hands again because I have to.

There's so much more to get my hands into.

<u>Sanity's Edge</u>

On the edge of sanity,

Lost somewhere between the myth and reality,

In a world of dream.

I see angels fly above me,

Demons lurking close beneath me, calling me.

Hear them taunting me?

I cry for help,

But no one hears,

Clock spiraling,

Speeding through the years,

Images of torture,

All my fears.

Sanity's edge,

Feel I'm standing high upon this edge

Looking down

Into my abyss in which I'll drown.

Out of control,

Preying on my mind, they've taken hold.

Sanity's edge,

Slowly being pushed off of my ledge,

Fighting this pain!

Racing through the sands of time,

There's no reason for this rhyme, and they're chasing me

Across this burning sea of glass.

Hands reaching out from everywhere,

Can't seem to waken from this nightmare, cross to bare,

Empty eyes that stare.

I cry for help,

But no one hears,

Clock spiraling,

Speeding through the years,

Images of torture,

All my fears.

Sanity's edge,

Feel I'm standing high upon this edge

Looking down

Into my abyss in which I'll drown.

Out of control,

Preying on my mind, they've taken hold.

Sanity's edge,

Slowly being pushed off of my ledge,

Fighting this pain!

I cry for help,

But no one hears,

Clock spiraling,

Speeding through the years,

Images of torture,

All my fears.

Sanity's edge,

Feel I'm standing high upon this edge

Looking down

Into my abyss in which I'll drown.

Out of control,

Preying on my mind, they've taken hold.

Sanity's edge,

Quickly being pushed off of my ledge,

Falling!

Falling!

Falling!

Falling!

Insane!

Bars and Scars

I look in the windows

As I pass the bars.

Faces laughing, singing.

They don't know the scars.

I'd stop in,

Maybe have a drink

Or two, or three,

If it would stop my think,

But that laughing,

That signing,

They won't ease

This pain lingering.

It will only

Make things worse.

That is the life,

That is my curse.

This sadness,

All this sorrow,

Is just for tonight,

Gone tomorrow.

It doesn't get me

Down for long;

Just one of those things

That comes along

From time to time.

Most times I smile

Because I know our

Time was worthwhile.

It's just on nights,

Nights like this,

While others drink

And lovers kiss,

Happily,

With their beer and wine.

I want what they have,

For just a time,

And they peer out

As the man passes,

My Guardian Anger

Raising toasts,

Clinking glasses.

Christmas, New Year's,

Joyous nights,

Raucous music,

Twinkling lights,

But I will have

A single lamp

Tonight, my eyes

A little damp,

A mixture of sadness

And memories:

Pictures, smiles,

Love and tragedy.

Tomorrow's sun

And cloudless sky

Will whisk away

This evening's lie,

And it's okay

To have a night like this,

Time to reflect,

To reminisce.

It makes me

Grateful,

Tears pour out

The hateful,

And I get the words

Out on the page,

Leaving love

Instead of rage,

And God knows

What my heart believes,

My dedication,

Wants and needs,

And I believe,

I believe, I believe!

And in the end,

It's mine to receive,

And I receive.

My tears are blessed,

And, tomorrow,

When I'm dressed

And have my coffee,

The world will be

Alright again,

And I'll be me, you'll see.

The scars,

They don't go away,

But sometimes you forget they're there,

Forget the pain,

But sometimes,

In February or November,

Sometimes,

Sometimes you remember.

Millions Fall

Millions fall,

God save us all!

We are at fault.

We've damned us all.

We created the pesticides,

Not thinking,

Not believing,

That we are the true pests.

Now we know,

And as the weeds grow

And enslave us with their limbs and thorns,

We watch nature reborn,

And it signals our demise,

So we can stop telling lies,

And then we have no more use

Because lies were what we were good to do.

We are and have been the profane,

Causing chaos and pain

When we could've, should've just refrained.

We had everything to gain

And everything to lose.

Now all we have left to do

Is to become extinct

And let the world get back in sync

And harmony,

The way it was always meant to be,

Only nature's symphony,

Without our useless, prideful soliloquy.

Forgive us, for we knew not what we did,

Not at first, at least I don't think we did.

Now is your chance to rid

Yourself of us, sons, daughters, kids.

Just do it! Pull the plug!

We are nothing more than thugs

Raping, destroying, pillaging,

Which we did most willingly.

Let the millions fall.

We don't deserve to be spared at all.

Take us down and then grow tall

And wipe out the remains of cities, walls,

Buildings, factories, houses, bars,

Trains, planes, buses, cars.

Without us, you could have the stars,

No more countries, no more wars.

Choke us down, choke us out.

Goodbye Mother Earth devout.

You'll have no more pleading from our mouths.

Forgive us, if you can, forget our cries, our shouts.

Goodbye, we were never worth

The pain of our birth.

Good, we leave you and go forth.

Goodbye our sweet blue Earth.

We never deserved you.

Don't Leave Me

Don't leave me,

The world is a better place with you in it.

Don't leave me,

My world is a better place with you in it.

Don't leave me,

I know this world is unkind.

Don't leave me,

You make it a little nicer.

I know the way you feel.

I know the pain you feel.

Don't leave me, don't leave me, don't leave me.

Don't leave me, don't leave me, don't leave me.

Don't leave me,

I know this isn't what you wanted.

Don't leave me,

I know it's not what you deserve.

Don't leave me,

God has a different plan for you.

Don't leave me,

He's not through with you yet.

I know the way you feel.

I know the pain you feel.

Don't leave me, don't leave me, don't leave me.

Don't leave me, don't leave me, don't leave me.

I know the way you feel.

I know the pain you feel.

I know the hurt is real.

I know, I know, I know, I know, I know.

Don't leave me, don't leave me, don't leave me.

Don't leave me, don't leave me, don't leave me.

It's not too late.

Don't leave me, don't leave me, don't leave me.

Don't leave me, don't leave me, don't leave me.

It's not too late.

Don't leave me.

Traces

Scattered bits of paper,

Ashes that flew out from the fireplace;

Can't really read the words anymore.

Don't really want to read the words anymore.

Torn pieces of pictures;

I could put them back together like a puzzle,

If I wanted to,

But I was the one who tore them,

And I don't need or want to see them again.

Old love letters,

Goodbye letters,

Pictures of happy times,

Mementos…

I don't need those.

Just traces

Of places and faces,

Alone in empty spaces.

I don't need those.

I don't need to reminisce,

I don't need to cry.

I've already said goodbye.

This painted rock with a heart that held your letter,

You could've done much better,

But now you'll never know how the story goes.

This is where it ends,

In cinders and ash

As I discard the past

And remove the trash.

They're just traces

Of places and faces,

Alone in empty space,

And I don't need those.

I'm realizing now that I never needed those,

And that's freedom.

Declaration of War

The time is now,

Armies on the move,

And every knee will bow.

It's time for you to choose.

Pick death or life,

Darkness or light.

Heaven or Hell?

Stand up and fight.

God's or the enemy's,

Whose side are you on?

I'm putting my foot down,

And I'm drawing the line!

This is a declaration,

A declaration of war!

Salvation, not damnation,

A declaration of war!

With sword and with shield,

The holy armor of God,

We will prevail

With staff and rod.

March into glory,

A battle already won.

Better choose wisely,

Spirit, Father, Son!

God's or the enemy's,

Whose side are you on?

I'm putting my foot down,

And I'm drawing the line!

This is a declaration,

A declaration of war!

Salvation, not damnation,

A declaration of war!

God's or the enemy's,

Whose side are you on?

I'm putting my foot down,

And I'm drawing the line!

This is a declaration,

A declaration of war!

Salvation, not damnation,

A declaration of war!

This is a declaration,

A declaration of war!

Salvation, not damnation,

A declaration of war!

Where Once My Angel Danced and Sang

Where once my angel danced and sang,

Wild flowers wither, like the pang

I feel in this hole in my chest,

Left to die like the rest.

Where is this love I was promised?

Why did I fall for words dishonest?

Though she never really told a lie;

She never really said goodbye.

The leaves here are all trampled down,

Crinkled, dried, and brown,

And spiderwebs begin to hang

Where once my angel danced and sang.

And spring's warmth changed to autumn's chill.

I've swallowed now this bitter pill

That she's forever gone, and still

I look for her beyond this hill.

Where once my angel danced and sang,

Below I heard the church bells rang.

It's like they're calling out for her,

But no reply comes in return.

I watch the skies and the river;

My breath in the cool air makes me shiver,

And I pull my jacket closer,

Nearly losing my composure.

Where once my angel sang and danced,

Where once we had our sweet romance,

There is nothing, nothing, nothing more,

Hardly life worth living for.

I don't know where, and I don't know why,

But she never really told a lie.

She never really said goodbye.

She just spread her wings…

Assault and Victim

You were not the one being tarred and feathered.

You were not the one being called heinous names.

You were not the one being hit, slapped, kicked.

You were not the one being spit on.

You were not the one sprayed with ketchup and mustard, on your
face, in your hair.

You were not the one having milk, flour, and salt poured on them.

You were not the one having to go somewhere else,

Sit somewhere else,

Eat somewhere else,

Live somewhere else.

You were not the one who had someone in their face,

Being yelled at,

Cursed at,

Threatened.

You were not the one who was bullied.

You were not the one being hurt.

You were not the one being killed.

You were not the one made to feel less than what you are,

Who you are,

Made to feel like an animal,

Or less.

You were not the one who was unwanted.

You were not the one who was beaten,

Whipped,

Raped,

Assaulted.

You were not the one who was assaulted.

You were not the one who was assaulted.

You were not the one who was assaulted.

No, you were just the one did all these things to someone else,

To others,

To others who were not like you,

Others who didn't look like you.

You did these things.

You did these things!

You did these things,

But you were the victim,

Weren't you?

They sat where you wanted to sit.

They ate where you wanted to eat.

They kissed who you wanted to kiss,

And you were mad.

You were jealous.

It was you who was the victim.

You, you, you!

You were the victim.

You were justified.

That is your narrative.

That is your truth,

At least what your little mind can fathom.

You were the victim.

You were right.

You were the victim.

You were the victim.

They sat and allowed it to happen.

They didn't talk back.

They didn't yell back.

They didn't fight back.

Yet,

You were the victim.

You were the victim.

You were the victim.

If say it enough times,

Maybe it will become truth.

You were the victim.

<u>I Was Holding A Cardinal Today</u>

I was holding a cardinal today,

Like everybody does.

I was sitting in the black metal chair on my front porch,

The one I got from my next-door neighbor after she passed away,

Only it was yellow then.

Weird that her family would put such a nice table and chars set out
by the side of the road for the trash to collect,

But I digress.

The cardinal was a male,

A vibrant red,

Beautiful.

He just stood there in the palm of my hand,

Twitching his head here and there periodically,

As cardinals do.

From time to time he'd look up at me.

I wondered what he was thinking.

What did he think I was?

Did he know I was just a man,

Or did he think I was some giant,

Or perhaps a god?

I am neither giant nor god,

But I guess it's all about perspective.

A nearby blue jay shrieked at one of us,

I don't know which.

Blue jays are like that.

I don't know if he was scolding me for holding the cardinal

Or scolding the cardinal for allowing itself to be held.

It wasn't the blue jay's business.

I didn't ask for its approval,

Nor did the cardinal,

But I guess the cardinal was embarrassed,

And it took flight,

Landing in the spruce tree near the house.

There's always some thing or somebody that delights in disruption.

The blue jay tittered about beneath that same spruce,

And I silently wished the cardinal would poop on the blue jay,

But it didn't.

The cardinal was better than that,

And I respect that.

I wish I was better than that.

I would've pooped on the blue jay,

But I can't climb the spruce.

Besides,

What would the neighbors think?

They can't mind their business either.

<u>One Day</u>

One day this will all go away.

One day this will pass.

You may not see the reason now,

But gray skies never last.

One day skies will turn to blue.

One day you will smile again.

Deep inside, you know it's true.

One day wind will chase the rain.

One day.

One day.

One day you will hear a word.

One day you may hear a song.

And you may then remember

The lies inside were wrong.

One day birds will sing aloud,

And food will once again taste good.

One day when your head is bowed

You'll feel the love you know you should.

One day.

One day.

There will always be a pain.

We have lessons to be learned.

One day you will smile again,

The blessings tears and faith have earned.

One day.

One day.

One day.

One day.

<u>When the Footprints End</u>

I woke up in the morning,

Saw the bed was empty,

And I panicked.

I threw off the comforter,

Pulled on my shoes,

And bolted through the open front door.

There was a single set of footprints in the mud that led down to the
beach.

I followed them,

Heart racing.

I could hear the surf and the sounds of the seagulls.

In the distance was a shrimp boat just leaving the docks.

I called your name,

And I startled and older couple who were walking their dog and
searching for shells.

Just past the dunes,

Your footprints were joined by a second pair,

Which seemed to come out of nowhere.

I was confused,

But I followed them.

The second set of prints was larger than yours.

Both sets led down to the water line,

Then turned north towards the pier.

I followed,

And soon the two sets of footprints merged into one,

The larger of the two.

I looked all around for your footprints,

But I couldn't find them.

I continued on,

Following the lone set of prints in the wet sand.

These led all the way down to the pier,

Then disappeared altogether.

I searched and searched,

Beneath the pier,

On the far side,

Closer to the water's edge,

Near the dunes.

There was nothing.

The footprints simply vanished.

You were gone,

And so was whoever you had been with.

I called out to the sea,

To the sky.

A dolphin surfaced about fifty yards out and went back under.

I looked for it but never saw it resurface.

I sat down in the sand by the pier,

And I looked out to the ocean for a long time,

Not really seeing,

Not really hearing,

Not really feeling.

I was just there.,

Just numb.

The tide came up,

Washed against my bare legs.

The water was cold,

And the smell of salt filled my nose.

It is time to go,

I thought.

It was time to go.

I stood and started back home,

The turned around to look at the sand by the pier once again.

The footprints had washed away.

They had all been washed away.

It was time to go.

I left my own footprints as I headed south,

Back the way I'd come.

<u>Grampus Krampus</u>

I was just a little lad

When I was told by my dear dad

The story of his dad, my grampus,

The one and only Christmas Krampus.

People think that he is bad,

But that just makes me very mad,

For Grampus Krampus is not a fiend.

He scares the children that are mean,

The bullies who pick on little boys

And the break the little girls' toys

And pull and pull their ponytails,

Making their little lives Hell.

Grampus has horns and a tail,

Cloven hoofs and fur that's swell,

A pointy tongue and sharpened fangs,

And he carries chains on which he bangs.

He carries branches that are made from birch

That he uses wo whip bad children first.

He has a bag to keep the children in,

The bad, bad children filled with sin.

He drags them to Hell or eats them whole

Without the need of plate or bowl.

Those wicked children no one needs,

The very worst, the wicked seeds.

My Grampus Krampus is the best,

But most of the year he needs to rest.

He's pretty busy at the Yule,

Punishing villains. That's pretty cool.

He's my hero, and I want to be

A Christmas Krampus, just like he.

So, be very good, be pure and be true,

Or one day we may come for you,

And you, and you.

Between the Razor and the Wrist

The hands shake,

This tip of the blade jerks,

Jabbing.

There is a drop of blood,

Then two,

And they run down the hand,

Dropping to the porcelain floor,

Red on white.

There is but a breadth,

A hair,

Between the razor and the wrist.

Scared,

But resolved.

What would it matter?

Stomach retches,

Heaves,

And the tears,

And the blood,

And the vomit mix.

The blade falls from his hand,

And the gleam of the silver reflects the bathroom light.

He drops to his knees,

Hands over his eyes,

Unconcerned about the mess on the floor.

Oh, God,

Oh, God,

Oh, God!

He looks at his wrists,

His arms,

His scars.

He has tried again,

And failed.

He always fails.

He will fail again.

<u>Speaking of Michelangelo</u>

The women were huddled in a group,

Smiling,

Laughing,

Pointing,

Talking.

I heard them speaking of Michelangelo.

I overheard them.

I eavesdropped.

They didn't notice me as I began to strip down.

Finally,

I stood before them,

As magnificent,

In my mind,

As David,

And I awaited their compliments.

They quickly got up and ran towards the exit.

I hurriedly bundled up my clothes and sped to the restroom to dress,

And to escape the glaring eyes from the rest of the room.

Perhaps I should have waited until the ladies had finished their lunch.

I will remember next time.

<u>Don't Need Us</u>

We are at the top of the food chain,

Numero uno.

We hunt,

We fish,

We grow crops,

We build,

We tear down,

We destroy,

We pollute,

We clean up,

We do it again.

Between humans,

We contribute,

We create art,

Music,

Literature,

But what do we contribute to the world,

To nature?

We set up nature preserves so that we don't kill what's there,

So we don't log what's there.

We keep the deer population down so they don't starve?

If we hadn't killed the wolves and the coyotes and the mountain lions,

They would've done that themselves.

What do we really do for the world?

We make noise.

We contaminate the air,

The waters,

The soil,

And we blame it on the cows.

We create trash,

And we burn trash,

And we bury trash.

We take and we take,

And we give nothing back.

We kill to extinction then cry for the loss.

We kill because we can,

Because we are the alpha,

The apex.

If we were to go away,

The earth would not mourn us.

The animals,

The plants,

The skies,

The rivers and the seas,

The mountains and the valleys,

That island of plastic…

They will all be reclaimed.

They don't need us.

They don't need us at all.

Inner Demon

Inner demon,

Scheming, screaming,

I introduce you:

He's waited so long to meet you.

How do you do?

How do you do?

He knows your lies and your truths,

And he knows mine,

And the miles and crossroads left behind.

He's very pleased to meet you.

A kiss on the cheeks,

The European way!

He's cultured and debonair,

Wouldn't you say?

Yes, I know his hands are warm;

They're for those long, cold nights.

You'll welcome them then without a fight,

That's right!

What did you expect?

My eyes and the bags beneath are tell-tale signs.

To you I bequeath him,

And him to you.

My mind is rotten,

But my heart is pure.

There is nothing more to say.

I have nothing more to give.

This is the only way that I can live.

I lay my darkness on the table for you to taste.

So sweet, divine, and chaste;

It's almost a waste,

But I leave you now as I walk away.

I'm sorry,

But my crimes are paid.

They are now paid in full.

I'm sorry.

I know what this is going to be like.

I'm sorry.

I'm sorry,

But he's waited a long time to meet you.

<u>No Stars</u>

The sun goes down,

And night begins.

I wish to see the lights,

The sights,

But there are no stars tonight.

There is a heavy fog

And a drizzling rain.

No twinkling stars

To ease this pain.

I just sit in the darkness and think,

Hands shaking, I could use a drink,

But I know,

I know,

That will do no good.

It will not bring lights to my neighborhood.

Not tonight,

But that's okay.

I will paint my stars on canvas

And wait for them another day

And any other time I need my stars

I will have them not too far.

On my canvas, black and gold,

Any time I'm feeling old.

When there's rain or snow,

And I'm feeling alone,

And there are no stars,

I can still have my own.

Innocent

We didn't do it,

Not us.

We've never stolen,

We never lied,

We've never sinned.

We're all innocent here.

We're all innocent,

Right, guys?

See?

We all agree.

Don't you see the purity in our eyes?

Do you think these lips could lie?

Cross our hearts and hope to die.

We would never, ever lie.

We are chaste.

We abstain.

We are free from blackened stain.

We only wear white.

That's our color.

That's how pure we are!

We never tempt.

We never fall.

We are innocent,

After all,

Innocent and pure,

Dainty,

Demure.

Weigh our hearts against feathers.

You'll see,

See how innocent we can be.

You know me,

Now look away.

Your eyes betray,

And I can't bear witness to that deceit.

We've had oil to anoint our feet.

I can't,

We can't,

Let our feet touch the ground.

It would sully our soles,

And we can't sully our souls.

No, no, no!

No anger,

No pride,

No gluttony,

No lust,

No envy,

No greed,

No sloth.

Sloths are too slow,

Anyway.

Go away,

And take down that mirror.

We don't need to see what you think you see.

Your eyes lie,

And we don't.

We are innocent.

We are innocent.

We are innocent,

And we'll keep saying that until you remember,

And recognize

We are not you.

We are innocent.

We are the innocent.

See the white we wear?

<u>Like I Hurt</u>

What were you thinking when you said the words you said?

Did you think about how I would feel?

Did you think they would cut me,

Hurt me,

Make me bleed inside?

Did you think at all,

Or did you just spout out words like you usually do?

These things I say to you,

These things I want to say to you,

These things I feel that wrench me apart,

That make my blood boil,

That make my pressure rise,

That make my head ache,

These things…

I won't say to you.

I will write them down,

And I will put them away.

I will tear them up.

I will burn them to cinders.

I will get them out of my head until the next time.

I am justified in feeling the way that I feel,

And I have every right to say the things I want to say,

But I won't.

I'm not like you.

I'm not evil and spiteful,

And,

Despite what you've said and done,

I won't do that.

I won't be like you.

I can't be like you.

I won't hurt you like you hurt me.

I don't want you to hurt like I hurt.

Nobody deserves that,

Not even me.

A Moment, Forever

A moment on the lips,

Forever on my mind.

A snip, a clip,

Are all that are left behind.

A smell,

A remembrance of a touch,

A life in Hell,

A heart with a crutch.

Wispy dreams,

Candles burn,

Frayed seams

And shadows everywhere I turn,

And I know I've learned,

And I remember,

Maybe not during the day,

But I do remember

In my dreams, the way

Times were,

And times passed.

I recall her

Face at last,

And I smile,

With a wrinkled eye,

And I can reconcile

My mind and heart with tears besides.

Fragments of life in lips,

Skin blemished and lined,

A moment, just a moment on her lips,

And eternity, forever, in my mind.

<u>Unmentionable</u>

You cannot speak its name.

You cannot speak their names.

If they hear you,

They will come,

And you wouldn't like that.

You can point,

You can write,

But don't even whisper.

Don't allow their name on your tongue,

From your lips,

For your sake.

They don't want you;

You're not worth their time.

Gods don't pay attention to rodents like us.

If you see them coming,

Just turn your back.

You don't have to cower,

You don't have to run,

You don't have to hide.

Just don't bring attention to yourself.

This isn't your state anymore.

This isn't your country anymore.

This isn't your world anymore.

Just shut up and look away.

That's what you should have been doing all this time.

Just shut up and look away.

Wolves Outside the Door

There are wolves outside my door,

And, though their fangs drip with blood,

They howl,

They cry out for more, more, more.

They never get their fill

From flesh, or booze, or pill.

They are frustrated,

As though they are never sated,

And they claw and claw

Until their paws are raw.

They want in,

With their awful, weeping din.

My hand is on the handle of the door,

Like so many, many nights before,

And the temptation is too much.

I can almost feel their lupine touch,

And my eyes roll back

As if under attack.

The wolves outside the door

Are preparing for war,

But I don't have the will to fight.

There's nothing left of my might,

And my hand shakes.

Here they are, my heart and soul to take.

I don't need them anymore, anyway.

Here I fall today.

Forgive this weakened man;

I have fought all I can,

But the howling and the clawing are so loud.

I go to the clouds.

My hand slowly, slowly turns the knob,

And face to face I meet my mob,

These wolves outside the door.

I am sorry, but I can fight no more.

Forgive me.

Forgive me.

<u>Savagery</u>

Descending into savagery,

The crimson, flowing imagery.

Descending, way too quickly,

Falling, stomach sickly,

Tasting mud and bile,

Feeling mad and vile.

There is red in my brain,

Electrical pain!

Nervous system overload,

Twenty terabyte download,

Too much information.

Take away this sensation!

Get me back to base,

Devoid this human race

And return to feral

Before this life turns sterile.

Savagery, my bite, my fangs,

Running with lupine gangs.

This is what's been missing:

Full silver moonlight kissing,

All snarls and howls

With no human prowls.

At last! At last!

The world has passed

And savagery rewarded,

Away from the sordid,

The dirt, the sleaze.

No filthy odor on the breeze,

Yet, the call me savage,

When all they did was ravage

The water, soil, and air.

Let them try to take me here!

I will show them the beast,

And we shall have a marvelous feast!

Tonight, perhaps, we dine,

Thee and thine,

Under the stars divine,

Thee and thine.

My savages, my soul;

Thank God for filling this hole.

This whole, my pack,

The savagery at my back.

Eternal, good,

My savagery, my brood,

My descent is complete.

No more need to compete,

And no more need of words or pen.

Here we begin…

<u>Your Air</u>

I want to breathe you in,

Feel you deep within,

Slowly exhale you,

Just to breathe you in again.

I want your scent.

I want to touch you,

Taste you,

Feel your breath,

Feel your air.

Let me drink you in.

One taste,

One breath,

And I will never go without,

And you will never want.

Your air is my air,

Mine is yours.

Breathe with me,

Love me,

Breathe with me.

The air is eternal.

I can whisper your name,

And a hundred years from now,

Someone will hear it in the breeze.

It will be an echo,

A memory,

But you'll live forever in the air.

Your air.

Your sweet,

Sweet air.

<u>Goodbye</u>

Nothing can prepare you,

Nothing can repair you.

Time to say goodbye.

Know I needed you,

Know I believed in you.

Time to say goodbye.

A reason, a season, a time.

A reason, a season, a time.

Thank you, my friend.

Time to say goodbye.

I didn't know you'd leave.

I didn't know when you'd leave.

Our paths crossed;

I may never know why.

Maybe I was changed,

Or maybe you were.

We were thrown together,

At that moment,

Without a coincidence.

It wasn't even a fork,

Maybe a four-way stop.

You went one way,

I another,

Neither one of us looking back,

So,

I don't even know which way you went.

I just know that you're not beside me.

For whatever I learned,

Whatever we were,

I thank you, my friend.

I love you, my friend.

It was time to say goodbye.

Down on Sycamore

It was down on Sycamore,

The house was numbered 804,

Red brick, shuttered, white upon the door.

Clotheslines hanging in the yard,

Bicycles with playing cards,

I was on my front porch playing cars.

Quite a long, long time ago,

Life was good on Sycamore.

Down, down on Sycamore.

Pine straw raked into a pile,

Road that seemed to go a mile,

Wearing clothes that had gone out of style.

Fried baloney sandwiches,

Didn't have all the riches,

If you acted up, you knew you'd get switches.

(And you'd never do it again).

Quite a long, long time ago,

Life was good on Sycamore.

Down, down on Sycamore.

We played barefoot in the creek,

Wave to everyone we'd meet,

Sunflower seeds or gum stuck in our cheek.

Life will never be the same,

Back then, life was pretty tame.

Our kids and grandkids think we're pretty lame,

But we know better.

Quite a long, long time ago,

Life was good on Sycamore.

Down, down on Sycamore.

Quite a long, long time ago,

Back when life was pretty slow,

Down, down on Sycamore.

Down, down, down on Sycamore.

Down, down, down on Sycamore.

2022

New Year's,

New tears,

New fears.

New smiles,

New styles,

New trials.

We meet each challenge headfirst,

Thinking of, but not fearing, the worst.

A new year full of promises,

Forget the Doubting Thomases.

We celebrate, and we will persevere

In the hopeful, blessed New Year.

Christmas Star

High in the sky

On this very night,

Something wonderful,

Something bright,

Something right.

Foretold in prophecy

For all the world to see,

This night would bring

The birth of a king,

And the angels sing:

Glory, hallelujah,

See the Christmas star,

The savior has come,

Born in a barn.

A light in the heavens,

A promise revealed.

Joy to the world,

Our souls will be healed,

Our hearts will be filled.

A son to a virgin

In a time long ago,

More than two thousand years

By the Christmas star's glow,

To pay the debt that we owe.

Glory, hallelujah,

See the Christmas star,

The savior has come,

Born in a barn.

Foretold in prophecy

For all the world to see,

This night would bring

The birth of a king,

And the angels sing:

Glory, hallelujah,

See the Christmas star,

The savior has come,

Born in a barn.

The savior has come,

Born in a barn.

ABOUT THE AUTHOR

Steve Cain is originally from Augusta, Georgia and now makes his home in New Richmond, Ohio with his wife, Theresa, his kids, Samantha and Ethan, three dogs, a cat, and a plethora of deer and turkeys. He is a Certified Safety Professional by day. His first book, *The Great Inevitable,* was published in 2019 through Losantiville Press. His last nine books are available on Amazon or through the author. You can connect with Steve on Facebook (Steve Cain Writer), on Twitter (@stevecainwriter), and on Instagram (19stevecain72). If you enjoy his writing, please leave a review on Amazon and Goodreads. Thank you!